THIS IS PLEASURE

THIS
IS
PLEASURE

Mary Gaitskill

Pantheon Books
New York

Copyright © 2019 by Mary Gaitskill

All rights reserved. Published in the United States by Pantheon Books,
a division of Penguin Random House LLC, New York, and distributed
in Canada by Penguin Random House Canada Limited, Toronto.

Pantheon Books and colophon are registered
trademarks of Penguin Random House LLC.

This book originally appeared, in slightly different form,
in *The New Yorker* (newyorker.com) on July 8, 2019.

Library of Congress Cataloging-in-Publication Data
Name: Gaitskill, Mary, [date] author.
Title: This is pleasure / Mary Gaitskill.
Description: First Edition. New York: Pantheon Books, 2019.
Identifiers: LCCN 2019033727 (print). LCCN 2019033728 (ebook).
ISBN 9781524749132 (hardcover). ISBN 9781524749149 (ebook).
Subjects: LCSH: Man-woman relationships—
Fiction. GSAFD: Suspense fiction.
Classification: LCC PS3557.A36 T48 2019 (print) |
LCC PS3557.A36 (ebook) | DDC 813/.54—dc23
LC record available at lccn.loc.gov/2019033727
LC ebook record available at lccn.loc.gov/2019033728

www.pantheonbooks.com

Jacket photograph of curled paper by Oote Boe
Jacket design by John Gall

Printed in the United States of America

First Edition

2 4 6 8 9 7 5 3 1

THIS IS PLEASURE

M.

I'd known Quin for maybe five years when he told me this story—really not even a story, more like an anecdote—about a woman he'd met on the street. Quin believed that he could perceive a person's most essential nature just by looking at him or her; he also believed that, in the same way, he could know what they most wanted to hear or, rather, what they would most respond to. He was a little conceited about these supposed special abilities, and that was how the story began. He saw a melancholy-looking woman, a "former beauty," as he put it, walking by herself in Central Park, and he said to her, "Aren't you the gentle one!" She replied, "And aren't you the perceptive one for seeing it!" After a few minutes of talk, he invited her to have tea with him. She agreed.

He didn't describe her further, other than to say that she was middle-aged and obviously lonely; she'd never been married, worked in PR, had no children. Even without a visual description, my sense of her was vivid: her slender forearm and long hand, the outline of her cheek giving off a subtle glow as she leaned slightly forward, into his attention, her mind quickened by this odd and unexpected man. And he would be leaning toward her, too. Quin was someone who *imbibed* people.

They exchanged numbers. I asked him if he'd told her that he was about to get married and he said no, he hadn't. He didn't plan to call her. It was enough to feel the potential between them, stored away like a cell-phone video of something that had already happened. "She would like being hurt, but very slightly. She'd want affection more. You'd spank her with, I don't know, a Ping-Pong paddle? And then touch her clit. *This is pleasure.*" He paused. *"And this is pain."*

When I repeated this story to my husband, he cracked up. We both did. For years after, apropos of nothing, one of us would croak, "This is pleasure"—my husband would make a perverted face and pinch the air—"And this is pain!" And both of us would crack up, just laugh our asses off. The whole thing was vaguely sadistic—so vaguely that it was ridiculous; clearly no harm was done.

"It wouldn't be a good outcome for her," Quin said. "She's open-minded but sensitive. I'm engaged to a much younger woman, and there wouldn't be any good place that it could go for her."

"She might've just wanted the experience," I said, "if she was lonely." I'm sorry to report that I said that. But I really thought it might be true.

They did speak on the phone, finally; she called him. He told her then about his engagement. He said that he'd like her to consider him a kind of guardian angel, psychically watching out for her. Which added to the hilarity for my husband and me. Even though it also added to the secret sadism. I laughed, but I wondered: Did the woman know, even dimly, that she was being toyed with? Did she feel that there was something wrong with the encounter, the way you might feel a mysterious hair drawn across your cheek? Why did I think it was so funny? It seems strange to me when I look back on it now. Because I don't want to laugh. I feel pain. Real heart pain. Subtle. But real.

Q.

Late at night, I went to my office for the last time. I was not allowed to go there during business hours and I didn't want to; it would have been unpleasant. The managing editor had instructed the security guard to let me in and see me out. Boxes had been packed and shipped already; before that, my wife had collected an envelope of emergency cash that I had left in a desk drawer. Even *she* didn't want to set foot in the office; the one sympathetic associate editor agreed to meet her and hand off the envelope at a subway concession stand—a pallid detail that serves only to underscore the level of revulsion Carolina feels about anything connected with my former professional life.

Anyway, I'd come one last time, to collect an orchid that had somehow survived months of inept watering and to see if any other tiny thing had been left behind. And one had, actually *two* had—though they were not that tiny, nor was I the one who had left them.

The first thing was my nameplate, strangely still affixed to the wall outside my office door, importantly announcing the existence of the now nonexistent QUINLAN M. SAUNDERS. It seemed like a nasty joke, and it was the sharp-browed and maybe pretentious "M," especially, that zinged me as I entered what had once been my office—where the second surprise sat quietly on my desk: a little cardboard cigarette box, its original graphic covered by a pasted-on image of a very red apple on a white background and, on the other side, the words "every day = choices," positioned like a brand name, in red and pink letters. When one opened the packet, one found not cigarettes but five very small scrolls of paper arranged with painstaking symmetry. Unscrolled, they read, in plain black type, "ugliness or beauty," "truth or lies," "courage or fear," "kindness or cruelty," "love or ____." The space for the last word on the last scroll was left blank. I didn't have to look; I remembered it tenderly well—as in when a doctor presses on your abdomen and asks, "Is it tender there?"

Years ago, I'd made this for a girl who still works in the row of offices opposite mine. A plain girl with short brown hair, bright eyes, and good coloring. Her body was thick-waisted but supple, with a peasant's grace—confident and humble both—and a quiet poise, greater than that of most beauties. Her eyes took in the world with passive depth and the occasional flash of mortal humor. She was intelligent, more than she realized, and I wanted her to learn how to use her intelligence more actively.

The cigarette pack came out of a hallway conversation we'd had about choices and opportunities. I spent several afternoons at my desk, piecing the little delicacy together in odd inactive moments. Strange and touching to remember the care I put into it, the sophistication and childishness, how I thought of it in her hands. I invited her to lunch to give it to her and, yes, I was right: when she saw it, that flash lit up not only her eyes but her entire face, and in that instant I became for her a magician who had given her an enchanted object. As if I *were* a magician, she listened to me tell her about herself: what she was like, what she needed, what she needed to correct. "We are going on a journey," I said, and we did. At the end of it, she had awakened to her ambition and learned how to satisfy it. As time went on, there were other girls I liked flirting with more. But for years—almost ten years—I kept our friendship alive with daily compliments and periodic lunches. I still have a handwritten note from her saying that our lunches were the "glory" of her week.

Now she had returned my gift not to me but to an empty room. Now she was one of my accusers.

I dropped the little box in a wastebasket on my way out, but then, because I did not want to leave evidence of such bitter feeling behind me, I turned around to retrieve it. I meant to drop it into a trash can on the street. But instead I took it home and put it in a drawer where Carolina would not find it.

M.

I met Quin when he interviewed me for an assistant-editor position, more than twenty years ago. At thirty-five, I was a little old for the job; I was coming from an East Village publication that was venerably outré, and was perhaps slow to realize that those two descriptors canceled each other out. Besides, it paid almost nothing, and I was looking forward to trading up. I had heard of Quin. I knew that he was English, from old-school wealth (father a banker, mother in organized charity), and that he was eccentric. Still, I was surprised by his appearance. He was at least forty, but he had the narrow frame and form of an elegant boy. His long brown hair fell over his brow in a juvenile style that was completely natural on him. His clothes were exquisite—simply cut, neutral colors, but finely tailored, soft, perfectly draped, nothing to stand out except the long silk scarf he wore, nearly always, around his neck. Without being beautiful, he gave an unexpected impression of beauty—but then he would subtly thrust out his jaw, with his lips parted so that his lower teeth were just visible, and his narrow face would look strangely insectile and predatory, like something with mandibles.

The interview was strange, too, whimsical and then unexpectedly cutting. He asked a lot of questions that seemed irrelevant and personal, including whether or not I had a boyfriend. He used my name more often than he needed to, and with an oddly intimate intonation that, in combination with his British accent, seemed not only precise but *proper*. That *proper* quality was somehow confusing: when he interrupted me to say, "Margot? Margot, I don't think your voice is your best asset. What is your best asset?" I was so discomfited and uncertain that I didn't know whether to be offended or not. I don't recall my reply, but I know that I answered abruptly and uncleverly, and then the interview was over.

I got another, better job, but still, when Quin's name came up in conversation, and it often did—he had a reputation that was somewhat notorious, yet unclear, as if people didn't know what to make of him, despite how long he'd been around—I vividly remembered his voice and my discomfiture and wondered why the feeling had stayed with me. And then, maybe two years later, I met him again, at a book fair in DC. I walked into some tricked-up rental location alone and saw him posing for a picture with two stylish young women, who were leaning on his shoulders, making funny faces and gangsta hand signs. He was looking at the camera, not at me, but as soon as the picture was taken he excused himself and came over to me. His voice was different this time—full of uncomplicated good will and so expansive that

I thought he was drunk, which he wasn't. He said that he was glad I was doing well, and, when I asked how he knew how I was doing, he said that he'd heard—"You bought a book I wanted, only a confident person would go for that book, I'm sure you know which one I mean"—but even if he hadn't heard, he continued, he'd have been able to tell by looking at me. The room was filled with the swift-moving noise of personality; somewhere in the background were a cake, bottles, and flowers. The gangsta girls gestured and grinned to each other delightedly. It all felt like a blessing.

Back in New York, we met at a restaurant that had once been a meeting place for the artistic elite but was now frequented primarily by tourists and businesspeople. We were seated at a deep banquette; Quin told the waiter that he wanted to sit on the same side as me, so that we could talk more easily, and then he was there, with his place setting. I'm sure he didn't say this right away, but in my memory he did: "Your voice is so much stronger now! You are so much stronger now! You speak straight from the clit!" And—as if it were the most natural thing in the world—he reached between my legs. "NO!" I said, and shoved my hand in his face, palm out, like a traffic cop. I knew it would stop him. Even a horse will *usually* obey a hand held in its face like that, and it outweighs a human by nearly a thousand pounds. Looking mildly astonished, Quin sat back and said, "I like the strength and clarity of your 'no.'"

"Good," I replied.

We ordered our meal. We talked about food. He again admired the novel I'd acquired, which had been turned down by every major house, including his, on the grounds that it was misogynistic (though, of course, *we* didn't call it that). He assessed the other people in the room, imagining what they did for a living and whether or not they were happy. I was unwillingly fascinated, both by the detail of his speculations and by how accurate they seemed. He paid special attention to a stout Japanese man who was lustily eating alone, legs spread proudly, one hand bearing food to his mouth, the other a fist on his splayed thigh; Quin said that of all the people in the room (other than me), this man was the one he'd most like to talk to, because he looked as though he were capable of "something great." But the main thing I remember from that night was the expression on his face as he retreated from my upraised palm, the surprised obedience that was somehow *grounded* and more genuine than his reaching hand had been.

I remember, too, a brief moment after dinner. He walked me home, and we said goodbye so warmly that a young man walking past smiled, as if touched by this middle-aged courtship. I went into my building and, halfway up the stairs, realized that I needed milk. I walked back out, to a corner deli. As I reached into the cooler for the milk, I glanced to my side and saw a funny man at the other end of the aisle, exploring his nose with a very large handkerchief while his other hand rifled through a shelf. His posture was intensely stooped, as if physically manifesting some emotional contraction. I was very surprised to realize that it was Quin—the posture was so radically unlike the elegant, erect stance I'd seen all night. He was so privately engrossed that he didn't see me, and I felt compelled to leave without buying milk, rather than let him know that I'd—what? Seen him explore his nose?

The next day, he sent me flowers and the friendship began.

Q.

I told Margot and I told my brother; I did not tell my wife. Not at first. I still had hope that it would blow over, or at least be handled quietly, and my hope was not unfounded. At first, the suit was not against me but against the publishing house, and all she wanted was a payment, which the company was prepared to make—as long as she kept quiet about her complaints. Her complaints were petty, absurd—which meant, as Margot pointed out, that they were almost impossible to keep quiet about.

"How would you enforce that?" she asked. "How would you even know what she was talking about at cocktail parties? Where else would she talk about it? Rape is one thing, but it's not like she can go to the media to report some weird thing you said years ago."

Margot was wrong. I felt that even as she spoke. But watching her, sitting squarely in her sense of reality, speaking confidently as she reached for the salt and lavishly poured it on whatever she was eating, I was reassured. I felt her love for me. Even though *she* was angry with me, too. She took the occasion to tell me how angry she was, and had been for years. "You treat people like entertainment," she said. "You joke and you prod just to see which way they'll jump and how far. You pick at their hurt spots. You delectate pain. It doesn't sound like this girl has a case legally, but, honestly, I can understand why she's mad. You didn't touch her, did you? I mean, sexually?"

I had not. Just sometimes on the shoulder, or around the waist. Maybe on the knee or the hip.

Affection. Not sex. "I so don't want Carolina to find out," I said. "She hates male oppression. Hates it."

And Margot laughed. *Laughed.* "Did you really just say that?" she said. *"You?"*

I said, "I'm concerned for my wife."

She stopped laughing. She said, "If it wasn't sexual, you don't have anything to worry about."

"But it could be made to sound sexual. Or just—she claims it cost her months of therapy bills."

Margot laughed again, more meanly—I'm not sure at whom.

"I'd like you to keep quiet about this," I said. "I mean, don't tell anyone. Not even Todd."

"I won't," she said. "Don't worry."

M.

I didn't tell that many people about him reaching between my legs. When I did, I told it as a funny story and mostly people laughed. But once someone, I don't remember who, said, "Why would you want to have a friendship with someone like that?" And I said something like "Well, he was very persistent and he can be a lot of fun." Which was true. But that was not why I came to love him as a friend.

For months, the friendship was almost entirely one-way, consisting of short, frothy e-mails from him, professional invitations, and phone calls to "check in." I didn't initiate anything until almost three months after our first dinner, and there was nothing frothy about the occasion. My boyfriend had left me for a girl in her twenties, my boss had been fired for publishing a memoir that she knew was a fraud, and my building was going co-op and I couldn't afford it. I was trying to get to my therapist's office when the subway groaned brokenly, stopped, grew dark, then hot, then seemed to die completely. Everyone on it was trapped, coughing, shifting, and muttering in the hot darkness for nearly half an hour before the thing reanimated enough to creep into the next station, where we were released to stampede up the stairs and fight over cabs. I lost that fight, and the loss was one ounce of pressure too many. I called my therapist to cancel, and then called a friend, who, incredulous at hearing me sob on the phone over a missed therapy appointment during work hours, said, "I'm busy!" and hung up.

It was all stressful, but scarcely enough to explain how I felt—as though a trap door had opened and I had fallen through it into scalding chaos, clutching at supports that came off in my hands, plunging, and transforming as I did into a mindless thing, a receptacle of fear and pain. Terrified by the sight of people moving all around me with energy and purpose, I sat down on the sidewalk and leaned my head against the wall of the nearest building. I sat there for some minutes, waiting for my heart to slow, and while I did I thought of Quin. I don't know why. But, when my heart had calmed sufficiently, I called him. He picked up quickly and brightly. I don't remember everything about the conversation, only that I said I was sick and worthless and "everybody" knew it. "Who is everybody?" Quin asked. "Just people," I said, "people I know." "How do you know they feel that way?" he asked. "Did they tell you?" "No," I said. "They didn't. But I can tell. I can just tell." When Quin spoke again, it was with surprising feeling. "I don't know who these people are," he said, "or why you would care about their opinion. But there is nothing sick or worthless about you. You are a lovely spirit." And, just like that, I stopped falling. The world and all the people racing through it became recognizable again. I was speechless with gratitude. "Don't bother with the subway," he said. "Take a taxi to my office. I'll wait for you downstairs. We'll go and have tea." And we did. There was no touching or talk about sex. We had tea and he listened to me and held my gaze with soft, attentive eyes.

Q.

If people could see the e-mails between my accusers and me, I believe they would be very surprised. My wife says, over and over, how "stupid" I was to send personal e-mails with any hint of flirtation from a company account. She never sends *any* personal communication from her work server, no matter how perfectly platonic. But, though I seldom engage with her when she's off on this tear, I believe that these e-mails are my best defense, even when they are a tiny bit sexy. Because they show mutuality, pleasure, even gratitude—friendship.

Caitlin Robison was my friend for eleven years. Yes, she was for a time an employee. She was even, to some degree, a protégé. But she was ultimately a friend. She came to parties at my home. She met my wife and child.

When Caitlin Robison came to work for us, she was twenty-four, a plain, dour young lady with a drab haircut (dirty blond) and a sexless style that I enjoyed teasing her about. I could sense that she was irritated by the teasing, but she was a good sport, which made me like her. Which she must've known, because within months she was teasing me back, calling me "straight fairy," "fop," and "buttercup"—saucy! She showed unexpected spunk, and when she tossed one of these cute *mots* over her shoulder, it made her angular ass seem somehow more round.

And she knew I was right. When she finally decided to do something about her hair, she asked me, "So, what do *you* think would look good?" She said it tauntingly, but I could see that it was a serious question, and so I answered it. She took my suggestion and her appearance improved by at least three points. Which was probably why, when I offered to accompany her on a shopping trip, she agreed *very enthusiastically*.

We didn't go anyplace expensive; she didn't make enough in her assistant's position, and anyway I prefer the charm of discount retail, even for myself sometimes. I'm a bargain hunter, and,

I discovered, so was she. Out of the office, as she pawed through sales racks and discount bins, her inner electricity switched on, and I could feel her motor. She was ambitious, this girl, vain and so practical that there was something squalid about it: this squalor was her sexiness. "How does this look?" she'd ask over and over, of some tight T-shirt or pencil skirt, and I would say, "Turn around, let me see." The fun of it was in her eyes as she searched my reaction and took her cues, and in the opinions she began to express. It was years ago, so I can't say that I remember what they were (except that she loved old *Ally McBeal* episodes, and could quote from some that were very sexual), but I remember their flavor. She talked about the man she was dating. I told her about my courtship of Carolina, our wedding. Afterward, I sent her an e-mail that said, "You plus me equals magic elixir!" And she answered, "Delicious!"

M.

We evolved this funny ritual, Quin and I. I am slightly afraid to fly and I went through a long period when I was *very* afraid. It was during this period that I began calling Quin every time I boarded a plane. I would ask him if he thought this flight would be all right, and he would say, "Let me tune in." There would be a pause, a sometimes lengthy one. And then he would say, "You'll be fine, Margot!" or "I *think* you'll be OK." If I couldn't reach him, I'd leave a message on his voice mail, and he almost always got back to me before the plane took off. On the rare occasion that he didn't, I would, on landing, receive a voice mail assuring me, "You're safe, love. Call me when you land." Once, when I couldn't reach him, I called Todd, the man I married, instead. Quin was outraged. "You called *him*? He doesn't know anything about planes!"

This was what he most liked: to give advice about the strange, small things that can sit oddly close to a person's heart, and sometimes press against it painfully. I could call him at any time and, if at all possible, he would drop whatever he was doing to give me advice about: whether or not to confront a friend about something that was bothering me; whether or not I should wear a particular style of makeup to a particular party; whether or not one of my husband's friendships meant that he was disloyal toward me. These conversations never took long, because Quin's advice was instantaneous, confident, and broadly philosophical.

I was not the only person who had this kind of relationship with him. I'd meet him at a restaurant, and he'd be getting off the phone with a woman who was crying about her husband's infidelity. I'd go to the theater with him, and he'd tell me that some girl was texting, wanting his opinion about something that her date had said. I went to his office and found him amid a crowd of girls, one of them weeping and crying, "Oh, Quin, I feel so humiliated!" And, in front of everyone, he advised her. Exactly *what* he advised, I don't recall. But I do remember the open, unashamed weeping, the placidity of the other women, the strength of Quin's voice, the room filled with sun, as if this were a sanctuary where every feeling might be aired and resolved.

Before the shit hit the fan, when I was feeling angry at Quin, I would sometimes look back on that moment and remember that feeling of openness, sunlight, and unashamed emotion. I would remember, too, the strange fun of our conversations about sex, him cajoling me to tell him about what I'd done or liked to do, me usually refusing to say but sometimes, for some reason, giving in. For example, on a long, boring train trip, he asked me if, during oral sex, it was important who came first and why. This turned into a longer conversation than you'd expect, and, even though I was careful with my language, in the middle of it, a roughly groomed older woman turned around in her seat and grinned broadly at me. I remembered talking to him on the phone before a party at his luxurious Central Park apartment, where I would, for the first time, meet his fashionista wife and their rich friends. I was worried about what to wear, and he said, "Anything you choose will be perfect. You're coming to the home of someone who loves you." I remembered him once talking about his daughter, Lucia, who was, at six, doing wonderfully adult drawings and writing poems that caused her to stand out even at the school for the gifted at which she was enrolled. We were in a taxi, and in the middle of the conversation he asked if he could put his head in my lap. I said, "OK," and he did. He said, "There aren't many people I trust enough to do this with." It wasn't sexual. I didn't pet his head or anything. He just lay across the seat with the back of his head on my thigh and quoted from his little girl's poems. It was nice.

There were many moments like that, not to

mention his ready professional and emotional support, for me and even for Carter, my fatherlessly depressed twelve-year-old nephew from Albany. During one particularly discouraging visit from the kid—I was single then, and did not know what to do with an angry twelve-year-old male—Quin spontaneously swooped in and commandeered the boy, taking him on an inspired tour of the Arms and Armor display at the Met, with a side trip to a video-game arcade. "He is *cool,*" Carter said.

Remembering those things, I would ask myself, *Why am I so angry?*

That was before. *After* the shit hit the fan, I looked back again at that moment of sanctuary in his office and contemplated: more than half of the women who were there had signed the endlessly circulating online petition, given interviews, demanded that Quin be fired, sought damages, made threats to boycott any company that would dare to hire him. They were angry, too.

Q.

It's true that I like to brag and I like to tease. And Margot, though very free in her view of sexuality, can be a bit morally stringent. I remember teasing Margot by telling her that I'd convinced a woman I'd just met, during a layover in Houston, to share with me what she thought about while making herself come. An amusing silence emanated from the phone, and then: "She didn't slap the shit out of you?"

"No," I answered pleasantly. "I was very polite. I led into it slowly. I was just about to get on my flight, we'd had a nice talk, she'd told me a lot about herself. It was just, you know, ships in the night, we won't see each other again, so . . ."

"I still don't understand why she didn't smack you."

"I can tell you why. She was a big woman, huge. Married to a professional football player—she'd told me that. I'm several inches shorter than she is, thin as a mantis, a pip-squeak. I'm in no way a threat to her."

Margot was silent; I could feel that her special brand of morality was offended by my ridiculous provocation. I could also feel her curiosity.

"And so many people, if they are honest, really want to answer those questions. You just have to ask in the right way."

"So she told you?"

"Yes. She told me."

Caitlin was a tease, too; that was part of our connection. I prefer not to speak of myself; it's generally not necessary. Most people are starved for perceptive questions, and the chance to discover their own thoughts. This is especially true of young women, who are expected to listen attentively to one dull, self-obsessed man after another. Caitlin was different. Where was it—at a book party at some nightclub or gallery chosen to convey a glamour that publishing rarely, or actually never, has—that she raised a glass of something pink to her mauve-tinted mouth and said, "You never say anything about yourself. You deflect."

"Not true," I replied. "I'm an open book."

"Bullshit," she smiled.

"Ask anything you like!"

There is some memory static here, possibly in the form of hors d'oeuvres offered by one of those handsome rental waiters who trail bruised dignity in their wake; perhaps she took so long choosing nothing that I thought she'd dropped the thread. But then she spoke seriously.

"How can I get to know you better?"

I was truly surprised and I answered without thinking. "How does a woman ever get to know a man?"

She looked so confused that I waited only a beat to answer for her: "Flirt with me a little more."

Her face abruptly froze. And then some people interrupted us, and our conversation ended with her expression wonderfully stuck on pause. It was either later that night or after some near-identical "event" that we shared a taxi and I asked her, "Don't you agree that sex is at the core of personality?"

"I don't know," she said. "People are complicated."

This was one reason that I liked Margot better. She was one of the few people who answered that question with an unhesitating yes. As did Sharona, from a completely different point of view. But Sharona was different in every way.

M.

The first time I was consciously mad at Quin was over something so trifling that I felt I was crazy. We were sitting down to a dinner party; he was, between snippets of table talk, texting advice to some girl who was upset because the guy she'd been dating wanted to see other women. "Do you think she should give him his freedom or say no, not allowed?" he asked me.

I said that I didn't know, that I didn't know her.

"I told her I'm asking Margot Berland, editor of *Healing the Slut Within*. She loves that book!"

I said, "I don't know her."

Food was passed around; conversations started. Quin answered a question from someone sitting across from us, then looked back down at his phone and addressed me sideways. "But you don't have to know her—it's an obvious question! Your boyfriend wants to see other people—"

"After how long?"

"It's been a few weeks."

"*Weeks?* I'd dump him."

"OK, I'm telling her, 'Margot Berland says—'"

"No, don't!"

"Why not? It would mean a lot to her that you—"

"It's her life—she should figure it out herself!"

Quin slipped his phone back into his pocket. "I already told her."

I sat there, inexplicably furious. Inexplicable because I'd been amused by and watched other people be amused by these—what a silly word and how accurate it is!—*microaggressions* ever since I'd known Quin.

And so *many* people had been amused, and not only from the publishing world. He gave huge parties two or three times a year, lighthearted, thrilling affairs that mixed people from the art world, movies, fashion, criticism, literature, medicine, and, more rarely, local politics. He'd occasionally invite a beautiful woman he'd met on the street that day and she would actually show up—stunned and stunning girls, barely out of their teens, from Eastern Europe or Africa, who barely spoke English but somehow trusted that this strange, slender man was worth their time. You never knew whom you'd sit next to—a handsome young hotshot running a phony pharmaceutical concern, a desiccated artist down on her luck, an elegant literary lady from Iceland—or what he or she might say. There was one regular, a young woman who wrote for an online art magazine; Quin had apparently invited her after she'd smacked him in the face a couple of times with a flyswatter, which she carried with her for a precise purpose—that is, to swat men who irritated her. When she came to the door the first time, Quin's wife, Carolina, greeted her warmly: "Oh, Miss Swatter, so nice to meet you. I've heard so much about you!" And, sure enough, the lady had brought her flyswatter with her; throughout the evening, she repeatedly swatted Quin in his own home, to his red-faced, beatific delight.

But Carolina wasn't always so easy or easily arch about her husband's odd relations with women. Maybe she never was. I met her shortly after she and Quin became engaged, when Todd and I had dinner with the two of them. She made a surprisingly distinct impression; she was an assistant editor at a fashion magazine, nearly twenty years younger than Quin, and I was not expecting to be impressed, except by her beauty. Of course she was beautiful, and very elegantly so. She was half Korean and half Argentine, and aristocratic on both sides; her family owned land outside of Buenos Aires. Her bearing was electric and deeply calm at once. She had a way of cocking her head that emphasized the purity of her facial lines, and the expression of frank, fascinated alertness in her long eyes accentuated their unusual shape (a teardrop, tilted up). She didn't say very much during the dinner, but she listened with erect intensity, as if her body were an antenna, and her up-tilted eyes and ears seemed linked, functioning as a single organ. She was a presence you took seriously, even if she barely spoke, even if she was only twenty-seven years old.

In spite of this impression, as the engagement became a marriage, Carolina quickly moved into the background for me, even when she made Quin a father. (He was ecstatic at this development, and every stage of it enchanted him; the flow of milk, his wife's new and natural tenderness. "I've never been that focused on breasts before," he actually *babbled* to me during a lunch, "but now I see them everywhere, love them, celebrate them, especially hers!") I saw her from time to time at parties and sometimes at readings, sometimes with her little Lucia, who was beyond striking, with her mother's pure-black hair and enormous anime eyes that seemed to be gazing into another, better world. Carolina and I were always cordial. Still, she surprised me one evening at an unusually casual dinner I had with her, Quin, and Lucia. The girl was five at that time, and she became very suddenly irritated with her father, to the point that she began to make a scene, even striking at Quin with her tiny fists. "She's overtired," Quin explained, and he decided, since they lived nearby, to take her home. When I wondered what had upset the child, Carolina shrugged.

"She's a girl," she said. "I don't think she enjoys watching her father flirt with every woman he meets any more than I do. Didn't you notice the way he was with the waitress?" She was in her late thirties by then and her fascinated alertness had been blunted, her erectness slightly compromised. But she was still electrically beautiful.

"Just so you know, that's never gone on

between me and Quin," I said. "He's a good friend. But nothing flirty. It's not like that at all."

And, so simply and sincerely that it astonished me, she said, "Thank you, Margot." Her husband had actually made this gorgeous woman, the mother of his child, jealous of a broad over fifty.

But I should not have been surprised. Quin was sometimes seductive with women who were older than me. We once went to a cocktail party given by a warm, well-exercised woman with wonderful deep lines on her face, disheveled gray hair, and confident red lipstick; she greeted Quin with an embrace that was nearly intimate and held hands with him while they spoke in confidential tones about banal subjects. They parted and, as we headed for the drinks table, he gave me a quick outline of her life: journalist, diplomat's wife, mother, environmental-cleanup volunteer. A few minutes into our drinks, he told me that the woman and her husband were still having sex, but only when the husband pretended to break into the apartment and rape her while she strenuously tried to push him out of her with her thighs and lady muscles. "I imagine she could almost do it," he said. "She's a strong gal and a fierce yogini!"

"Did it turn you on to hear about it?" I asked.

"No. Not especially." His tone was dry, nearly judicial. "But it interests me. It helps me understand her. Knowing that, I feel I'm better able to help her with her marriage. They've been having trouble lately."

He said this with perfect seriousness.

Q.

Sharona was a girl straight out of the fifties. She even dressed that way, and not self-consciously. I never saw her in pants; she wore skirts and dresses exclusively, modestly cut but given a sexy edge by her high-heeled shoes and boots. Her hair and nails were flawless. She had a heart-shaped face and big dark eyes with a secret expression that wanted to be released—there was something intense and seeking in her gaze. She wasn't a real beauty, but she had a beautiful laugh and even a beautiful frown. For her, sex *was* the core, and that was why she refused to speak of it or evoke it with her presence; for her, the core was "sacred." She used that word during a conversation at a bookstore after a reading. I'd asked about her boyfriend, the most innocent question first, but, where most girls would begin to trust me or try to impress me, she looked at me with mild reproach and said, firmly, "That's inappropriate." Still, the soft directness of her eyes and voice was more intimate than my question. I asked her if she was religious and she laughed before saying no. I asked her if she prayed. Her expression shifted, a depth change. "Yes," she said, "I do." I told her that I prayed every day. I said, "When I want to find out what someone is really like, that's one of my first questions—do they pray?"

"You want to know what *I'm* really like? You just met me."

"I prefer to know whom I'm talking to, yes." We spoke of the writer who had read his work—a poseur, she thought. I disagreed, but not too strenuously. I asked if there was anyone in the room she'd like to meet. She said, "Not especially."

She accepted my invitation to lunch, then and many times after. She enjoyed talking about books. She enjoyed my appreciation of her mind, which was sincere; she was a delicate and nuanced *perceiver*. She had a dull assistant's position at an art magazine that reviewed books (I knew her boss, an unpleasant fellow), and I could feel her pleasure when she was able to flex her intellect. Not ostentatiously but quietly, firmly. And she realized, I'm sure, that I was a good person to cultivate.

Caitlin and I had been friends for some time by then, but the friendship had become intermittently hard and sparring—nasty, even. She was in love with a man who seemed to despise her; it was plainly a delusional crush, and I encouraged her to drop it. When she insisted on the legitimacy of her feelings, I said that, if it was really love, she should pray to know what was right for both of them and then act on it. Every time I saw her, I'd remind her to pray about it.

The outcome was predictable—the usual dreary disaster. She seemed to blame me for it; I can only think this was because I had witnessed her slow-motion humiliation. Even when she found a new boyfriend, the bitterness of that rejection stayed in her heart and made her act strangely around me. She invented a little game: If I had to wear a button with a single word to announce who I was, what would it say? *Flaneur? Voyeur? Creep?* The severity of the word she chose varied from day to day, as did the "buttons" I chose for her: *Narcissist. Opportunist. Crybaby.* I remember her smiling as if drunk during these exchanges, and, even though I was never drunk, there was a feeling of intoxication in our bitch-slapping.

Anyway, we continued to have lunch and to confide in each other. She accepted my professional advice (I was a great help to her), and she, in time, advised me about Sharona. Eventually, I helped her get a plum job with a literary agency. On her last day at the office, she wanted to know if I'd still invite her to my parties. I said, "As long as you flirt with me, love." And we did continue to flirt, though mostly via e-mail. Had lunch every now and then. I didn't invite her to a party, though. There were others who better filled the spot that she had occupied.

M.

There are so many funny/awful stories that it's hard to stop telling them. The nineteen-year-old who texted him every time she (a) took a shit or (b) had sex with her boyfriend. The girl who texted him to describe her fantasies every time she masturbated ("OK, it's hard to type right now, because my hands are shaking . . ."). The time we attended a reading by a young female writer and Quin, on being introduced to her, stuck his hand in her face and said, "Bite my thumb." The self-possessed young woman looked at him with disgust and turned her back. I said, "Why did you *do* that?" He wasn't fazed. "She's cute," he said. "But she's not game." He shrugged.

Grotesque, but at the same time paired with such peculiar, delectating joy. Once, when my husband and I were feeling down, we talked about how everyone we knew seemed ultimately unhappy, or at least discontented. "Except Quin," I said. "Except him," Todd agreed. And, putting on his Quin-the-pervert face, he quoted, *"Where the bee sucks, there suck I!"* We laughed, then sat there, contemplating Quin's abnormal happiness.

And why wouldn't he be happy? He had a gorgeous wife and an exceptional child, and he was an excellent editor, who published some of the best writers of the moment. They tended to be clever niche writers rather than heavyweights, but the quality was undeniable and some of them had devoted followings. Many of them were writers whom no one else in publishing had believed in at first. Quin did believe, passionately, even *morally*:

"She's marching for goodness," he might say, or "He's marching for sexuality" or "marching for truthfulness." (Morality was, oddly, important to Quin. He analyzed and criticized people based on their moral traits; "self-centered" was one of his harshest accusations—an irony, given how much he encouraged people to talk about themselves.) Quin would take up these marchers, pay them advances that were all out of proportion, and exult when they succeeded. Which happened often enough that even writers whom *everyone* believed in—that is to say, bid on—finally came to him too, without his making much of an effort to land them.

I remember going with him to a publishing party for one of them, a young black man ("Marching for justice with humor and style!") whom Quin had positioned for celebrity. The party was held in an art gallery that was showing work by someone who painted imitations of hoary masterpieces, in which she had replaced the original Caucasian figures with famous people of color. I met Quin in his office; I was wearing a skirt and heels and carrying a shopping bag and a little purse. He insisted that I let him carry the shopping bag, because, even though I would check it at the door, he thought it spoiled my look—*plus* he would enjoy being "at [my] service." I agreed, and then he said that he thought I should also dispense with the purse, because, although it was small and very nice, it made me look less free. "But I need it," I said. "I've got my wallet and lipstick in there."

"Then let me carry them," he answered, "here." He indicated an inner pocket of his jacket.

I hesitated.

"You're effervescent tonight," he said. "But that purse takes something away. It makes you more mundane, less delightful. I want to see you walk through the room giving off an aura of freedom."

I said, smiling, "But if I give you my wallet I'm not free. Because you've got my wallet."

He was right, though. I would have looked and felt more free without the purse. Especially while we were dancing; there was a good DJ, and we danced for hours.

Q.

When Caitlin left, a girl named Hortense took her quasi-secretarial position. Caitlin recommended her, in fact; I don't remember the connection, but somehow they knew each other. Truthfully, I liked Hortense better; she was more confident, less ambitious, prettier, altogether a finer creature (huge dark-blue eyes; plump, tiny mouth; graceful neck; curly hair; musical voice). I suppose out of habit I contrived for us to go on an occasional shopping trip, and, perhaps because of Hortense's wonderful prettiness, I was drawn to stores that were a bit more upscale. On our last such expedition, she tried on a T-shirt and let me come into the dressing area to see what it looked like on her.

There she stood, young, brimming with confidence in her allure, glowing in the expensive light. The shirt fit her perfectly and I meant to say that. Instead, through cloth and bra, I reached out and touched her breast, circling the tip with my finger. Neither of us spoke. I don't remember the look on her face, just my finger moving and her nipple responding, hardening. Magic elixir. Delicious.

The moment lasted seconds, and then I bought her the shirt and we went on with our afternoon. But the relationship shifted slightly, becoming closer, less a flirtation and more a true, sweet friendship. By some tacit understanding, we did not go shopping again and I never touched her again in quite that way. But at lunch, sometimes, or even in my office, we held hands while we talked. I liked that a lot.

It was probably foolish of me to tell Sharona about this incident, but I wasn't thinking that way then. I wanted to challenge her; I wanted her to understand. We were talking about the word "sacred," what it meant to her. It meant something beyond words, she said. Something that was beyond the quotidian, but was expressed through it. I agreed. And then I told her what had happened between me and Hortense. I said that it had been, in a small way, sacred to me.

Her face became very still, her eyes wide. She asked me what Hortense did at the publishing house. How old she was. Would she continue working there? And, finally, "Why was this sacred to you?"

"I don't know, exactly. Like you said, it's beyond words. But I felt it. Awe at her beauty and at being alive. And that this strange thing could happen. Going up to the very line of acceptability and not crossing it."

"How do you think she felt?"

"Maybe a little of the same. Not enjoying it, exactly. But willing. Understanding my need." I told her that I didn't think it would happen again, and that was part of what made it special. I asked her if she understood that.

She was slow to answer, but finally she said,

· 50 ·

"I guess I do. But I hope you understand that it would never be OK to touch me that way."

"Never," I said, honestly. "I would never touch you that way." I reached across the table and took her hand. We sat like that for a moment, her captive hand softening incrementally. I turned it over and resisted kissing it. The check came. It was a victory, I thought.

M.

It's odd to me that, although Caitlin was the one who finally . . . *broke* Quin, I never heard about her. I don't think I met her, either, and I met countless young women in Quin's orbit. I *did* meet Sharona once, and heard about her even more. (*Wasn't she innocent? Wasn't she special? Wasn't she straight out of the fifties?* Though she was clearly just a standard nineties girl, right down to her silly pop-song name.) Toward the end of their "friendship," he actually sent me texts that he wanted to send to her, asking my opinion on them. Some of these texts were aggressively teasing; some were nearly pleading, including one in which he compared her refusal to "share" more of herself to the Republican Congress's refusal to share societal wealth. (That one I definitely told him not to send.) We could spend whole lunches analyzing her behavior, particularly why she wouldn't let him stroke her back or even take her elbow to guide her through a room. It was the same conversation, over and over: I lectured about respect and boundaries; he wondered how someone could be so "precious" about herself and declared that he would *never* refuse the needs of a friend. I retorted, "What if I needed you to kneel down and kiss my feet every time you saw me?" He said that he would do it. I said that it could be very awkward. He said that he would do it right there, and then he actually knelt on the floor of the restaurant; when people stared, he explained, "I'm honoring the needs of my darling friend." He actually tried to kiss my feet. I had to say "Stop!" But I was laughing.

I heard all about Sharona. But I didn't know about Caitlin until the lawsuit. "What did you do?" I asked. "Why do you think she is so angry?"

He shrugged. "She asked what she had to do to get invited to my parties and I told her she had to flirt with me more. I think that really offended her."

Of course, the stories in the paper listed many more offenses, including sending Caitlin, while she was still working for him, a video of a man spanking a woman. People were shocked when I showed sympathy for him on that one. I said, "I know it sounds terrible. But I don't think it really happened that way. He probably asked her what she likes to do sexually, and she told him she likes spanking. For him, it'd be the most natural thing in the world to send her a spanking video. Yes, it was still rude!" I admitted. "But—"

Quin said, "I didn't even ask. She told me on her own. And it wasn't porn or anything—it was

John Wayne spanking an actress in some old-timey Western!"

Caitlin wasn't even the one who accused him of actual spanking. Someone else revealed that, in an interview with the *Times*. That woman wasn't actually part of the lawsuit, but she certainly made it look reasonable.

Q.

If my wife stays with me, I can get through this. I can get through it regardless, but . . . *broken, hobbled, without her respect;* these are the kinds of words that can pile up on one another when my mind goes in that direction, so I don't let it. I take my morning run. I keep my head up. Bright light fills my mind. Life is a miracle. It goes on, no matter what happens to one selfish man. "You are Quinlan Maximillian Saunders, and through this you will find a better place." Carolina said that to me at two in the morning, holding me in her arms, with tears streaming down her face. Earlier that day—technically, the previous day—she'd slapped me publicly, in the street. She did this because I'd seen one of my accusers, smiled at her, and said, "Hello."

"She smiled at *me*," I explained. "I was just smiling back." And my wife turned and hit me. As hard as she could, with her open hand.

"Idiot," she said. She spoke calmly and quietly, though loud enough for passersby to hear. "I guess I can't let you out, even with me."

Later, she held me in her arms. But it is in fact the case that she forbids me to go out, and I go along with it because I know what this has done to her, and what she thinks it will do to Lucia one day—although I think Carolina underestimates the child.

It's so terrible and so absurd. Absurd that I did certain things, yes. Absurd, too, that Caitlin holds a position that I helped her get and, from that position, accuses me of things that she was party to. Even more absurd, she is called "brave" for it.

And, finally, I find it just slightly absurd that what has hurt Carolina the most in all this, I suspect, is not a wound to her heart or even to her true dignity but to her social identity: she went from being the wife of a respected editor to being the wife of a pariah.

"What kind of wife am I?" She screamed these words in the presence of one of my closest friends. "What kind of wife will I be for the cameras? At the court date? A loyal wife? A spiritual wife? A humiliated wife?" She *screamed,* my elegant, formidable Carolina, and my friend and I just sat there, gaping at her pain.

"It's me who has to call the lawyers," she ranted, "and the publisher who stabbed you in the back after you fell on your sword for him. It's me who has to get on the phone and remind the hypocrite that without you he has no scapegoat, and without him we have no insurance."

"Can you countersue?" my friend suggested weakly. "Can you take the girl to court or—"

"Are you kidding? Do you know how much

that would cost? Do you know how much we've lost already?" But she at least stopped shouting. "I don't care about the girl. I care about health insurance and survival for my family. I don't care about vindication. I don't want to win. I just want my family to be OK."

Terrible. Not absurd. Terrible. I feel it. I feel it every day. But I don't think about it. It hurts too much to think about it. Instead, I think about Sharona. I even wrote her a letter. I don't know if I'll send it. Margot said that it wouldn't make any difference; if that's true, I might as well:

I read in the amicus brief that you were among those offering your experience with me as an example of my abusive behavior. I am shocked and hurt by this. I never intended any pain or disrespect. I teased, maybe too much. But you must know how much I valued our friendship and respected you. I offered to include your boyfriend in our circle just to be in your presence. Please,

Sharona, don't be part of this. I'm not asking because I think it will affect the legal outcome—I know that it won't. I'm asking because it truly hurts me to have your name in any way connected with this. Please show me a fraction of the regard I feel for you.

I was very tempted to add that Hortense, the sacred dressing-room girl, was adamantly not a part of the lawsuit, that she had even sent me a supportive note. (Which was especially meaningful considering that Hortense knew Caitlin; I wonder how that friendship is going?) But I didn't.

M.

"You had a paddle in your office? Just lying around? I never noticed that."

"Oh, Margot, stop it. It was more like, I don't know, a serving spoon or a spatula."

"And it just happened to be in your office. And you—"

"We had a lunch date and she was half an hour late. I hate it when people are late. I'm sure you've noticed that I'm very punctual."

"Yes, I have."

"So I was a little bit annoyed and, almost to make the situation lighter, I said, 'Don't you think you should be punished for being late?' And she said, 'I guess so.' So I said, 'What should the punishment be?' I had no idea what she'd say. She said—no, she didn't just *say* it—she turned around and bent over." He turned and showed me, his butt presented with knees and thighs pressed primly together. I think he even put his hands on his knees. "And she said, 'A spanking.' So I swatted her once with this butter knife—"

"You said spatula."

"Whatever it was, I don't remember. And then we went to lunch and had a great time. And now she's saying that I beat and degraded her."

I face-palmed as I pictured it: the breezy ambience of the office, the light words, the girl maybe tossing a little moue over her shoulder as she playfully presented her ass; perhaps she started at the stinging sensation, but then—off to lunch and laughter! And then the silent subway ride home, across from a row of tired, distracted strangers staring at their phones, or just staring.

"This is what I don't understand. It was her idea—no, it *was* my idea. But she more than went along with it. She didn't have to stick her ass out. She didn't have to do anything. None of them had to."

"Quin," I said. "I would never say this in public. I wouldn't say it to anybody but you. And maybe Todd. But listen. Women are like horses. They want to be led. They want to be led, but they also want to be respected. You have to earn it, every time. And they are as strong as fuck. If you don't respect them, they will throw you off and prance around the paddock while you lie there bleeding. That's what I think."

Q.

Do I respect women? If I'm being truthful, I'm not sure I can answer generally and in all cases. But I can say this: I respect my wife. And I did not betray her.

"I flirted. That's all it was. I did it to feel alive without being unfaithful. I never—"

"It would've been more dignified if you had," Carolina replied. "It would've been more normal."

"It would be more dignified if I'd been *unfaithful*? Do you mean that?"

She sat very straight, looking out our big, west-facing windows. Countless rectilinear shapes, silver and gray, rose in an abnormal sky of purplish clouds and freakishly pink light. An especially vertiginous beauty of glass and steel caught the sunset and turned orange.

"You're not even a predator," she said quietly. "Not even. You're a fool. A pinching, creeping, insinuating fool. That is what's unbearable."

M.

I didn't know most of the women who had spoken out against Quin. But I knew one, a novelist named Regina March, one of his minor discoveries from some years back. I'd seen her at Quin's parties and liked her; she was a warm, opinionated forty-year-old, who, I remember, always hugged Quin goodbye. I was astonished to see that she was one of hundreds of women who'd signed the petition naming multiple "abusers" and demanding that no one ever hire them again; they specifically threatened to boycott any publishing house or media company that did hire one of them. Essentially, this intelligent, delightful woman was threatening the livelihood of the man who'd first published her!

My astonishment must have shown when I saw her at a party; her face fell at the sight of me. Provoked by her guilty look, I slowly pursued her around the room, joined her in a three-way conversation, and politely awaited my moment. I didn't have to wait long. As soon as the other woman walked away, she looked at me with emotional eyes and asked, "How is Quin? How is Carolina?"

"As well as you would expect," I said.

"I think of them every day," she said. "I've wanted to reach out but I—"

"*Reach out?* You wanted to *reach out*? My God, Regina, why did you sign that thing?"

She started to cry. She said that she hadn't seen his name on the petition until after she'd signed it—there were so many names—and because it was online, she couldn't unsign it. Maybe his name was added after she signed it? Because if she'd seen it she wouldn't have done it! Could I tell him, could I tell Carolina, could I—

Q.

After my case has been dismissed—and I feel there is a good chance of that happening—I want to make a statement. I'll write a blog, maybe, or send something to the *Times*. Maybe I'll just read it in court. The idea came to me late one night—early morning, really, probably around four, when I woke with my heart so low in my chest that I could barely feel it. Carolina was next to me, and, though I wanted to press against her for strength, I lay still. Her features were barely visible in the dark, but I saw the contours of her forehead, lips, nose, and cheek; these shapes expressed sadness and helplessness, but her curved shoulders and her neck declared animal determination *to push through this shit*. Carolina: the sacred figure behind the gaudy tapestry of my public life. Unable to help myself, I moved closer and, coming into the area of her warmth, was flooded with relief and residual happiness. Then she moved, in her sleep, away from me.

I thought, *I've got to do something. I have to fight somehow. I could check in with old friends in London. Maybe the poison hasn't spread there. Terrible to have to face my father, but . . .* I rose and went into the living room and looked out at the park, with its deep vegetable greens and rough browns under the colorless sky. But I didn't want to go to England; I wanted to stay here. A few cars moved sluggishly in the street; a horse-drawn carriage humped along at the curb. Sounds came up—a garbage truck, a bus, something large beeping horribly as it turned, the gray noise of traffic. Horns, blaring and bright then soft around the edges, subsiding into the dominant gray. Beautiful from here—the obedience to the grid, the vying against it. It gave me faith in myself. Words and music flowed freely in my mind, coming, it seemed, from a place of deep subterranean order, a place from which the signs and symbols of society draw their vitality.

Buoyed by the ramshackle order of the waking city, I felt that all could be well, that I could make myself understood, and—perhaps—even make peace with those who had felt wronged by me.

I sat down at my desk and wrote:

> I realize that the way I've carried myself in the world has not always been agreeable to those around me. I come from a generation that values freedom and honesty above politeness, and I have acted from those values, sometimes as a provocateur, even a trickster. Maybe I've gone too far sometimes, been too curious, too friendly, at times a little arrogant. But

From there, I didn't know what to say. I found myself strangely distracted by memories of a visual artist who'd been a frequent guest at our parties, a sexy girl who'd recently dropped me a sweet e-mail. I thought of a video she'd made of a man kneeling and barking at her command; she'd made him bark for a kiss ("Louder! More!") until they both collapsed in fits of laughter. With some effort, I returned my feelings to my wife and to Lucia, who had awakened from a bad dream a couple of nights before and climbed into bed between us, wanting us both to hold her. But, even though it had happened recently, the memory felt distant and somehow made it harder to write the statement. I sat there for another hour, and still I did not know what else to say.

"I think it would be good if you started with an apology." That's what Margot's husband, Todd, suggested when I asked them for help with the statement. We'd had drinks and a discussion in their old-school Brooklyn apartment—a warren of little rooms redeemed by an expansive kitchen that was charming, even with its broken molding and stained, sagging ceiling.

"Apology for what? Being myself?"

"For causing pain. I realize that some of them are overreacting or just jumping on a trend. But some of them must've been genuinely hurt and—"

I love Todd. He is a kind and earnest man with slightly strange proportions—small hands, delicate mouth, formidable shoulders, and a large and somehow senatorial head. I love him as a loyal dog to Margot's skittish cat. But I am not a dog, and it won't do for me to pretend that I am. "But I don't believe they were hurt. They were maybe offended, but that's different."

"But would *they* say they were hurt?"

Margot didn't give me time to answer. "I would say that you don't understand why these people are saying these things when they acted like they were your friends and accepted favors from you."

"I don't want to say, 'I don't understand.' That's weak and whining. And besides, I *do* understand."

"What do you understand?" she asked.

What patronizing patience from my darling friend! Still, I answered calmly. "That this is the end of men like me. That they are angry at what's happening in the country and in the government. They can't strike at the king, so they go for the jester. They may not win now, but eventually they will. And who am I to stand in the way? I don't want to stand in the way."

They looked at me with bleak respect.

"They were my friends. I would still be friends with them. I miss them."

"Friends?" Margot really did *sneer* at the word. "That little bitch ruined your life!"

"She did not ruin my life. I would never give her that power. She's just a confused kid!"

Again they looked, simply bleak this time.

M.

"He wants to be friends with them," Todd said incredulously.

"I know."

"He's fucked," Todd said.

"I know."

"Imprisoned in a cloven pine."

"What?"

"And in their most unmitigable rage into a cloven pine, within which rift imprisoned he didst painfully—"

"Oh stop, this isn't Shakespearean, not even a little. And don't compare the women to witches."

"Why?" He was doing the dishes as we spoke, and turned to look at me. "You just called one of them a 'little bitch.'"

He looked genuinely confused, so I just said, "I know," and we dropped it.

But his comparison wasn't right. Ariel didn't pinch Sycorax's ass or tell her to bite his thumb. Ariel was punished for refusing to obey the witch's commands; Quin was being punished for issuing commands. Or at least that was how the women had responded—as if they had been given commands by someone who had the power to do so.

This is where I don't understand my own feelings. When I say to my colleagues that the women should have just told Quin to stop, that *I* had told him to stop and had *made* him stop, they inevitably tell me that the power was disproportionately his, and that even if *in theory* the women could have pushed back they should not be expected to, they shouldn't have to. I get aggravated then and splutter about female agency versus infantilization, etc. I say, yes, he acted badly. I was angry at him, too. But did he deserve to lose his job, his right to work, his honor as a human? Did he have to be so completely and utterly crushed? Couldn't people have just made fun of him for being a dirty Jiminy Cricket and left it at that? (A sweet cricket, crossed with the wicked Foulfellow fox—*hi-diddle-dee-dee!*)

But there are other things I don't say, can't say. And this is where the heart pain comes. Subtle. But real.

A few years ago, Quin told me that a friend of his was experiencing recovered memories of childhood sex abuse. He was skeptical of this process and so tired of the subject that he found himself avoiding her. "Quin," I told him. "If you care about her as a friend, suspend your skepticism. Even if it sounds like bullshit. This is important and she's trusting you." And, to make him understand the strength of my feelings, I told him that I'd been abused as a five-year-old.

"And you remember it?" he asked.

"Not all of it. But I remember some of it very vividly. It was shocking, in every way. The powerful sensation of it. He didn't hurt me physically, but it was like being stunned by a blow and then mesmerized. The sensation was too much, too strong for me at that age."

"Who was he?"

"A friend of the family. I remember his large, dark shape. I don't mean that his coloring was dark. There was a dark feeling about him that I could somehow see. A feeling of pain. I remember climbing in his lap and trying to comfort him."

"I'm sure you did comfort him. You must've been a little angel to him."

"Quin," I said. "That's a weird thing to say."

"Why? Children can be powerful. I'm sure you took away the pain for a little while."

"Not for long. He killed himself."

"Terrible. Still, I'm sure you helped him."

And then the conversation moved on. I didn't feel anger. I don't remember what I felt, exactly, except a strange, muted combination of incredulity and acceptance. It didn't occur to me to say anything to him about it until much later. He didn't remember the conversation, but he apologized anyway; he didn't understand why I was upset. "I was just trying to find something positive in it," he said. And I imagine that was true. But inside I stayed angry. At the same time, I still loved him. I still leaned on him for support and counsel. I was like the women who didn't stop him and who acted like his friends even as they grew angrier and angrier. It wasn't because he had more power than I did; that didn't really matter. And it wasn't because I'm like a horse. I don't know why I behaved the way I did, and I kept doing it; *he* kept doing it. The little jabs and jokes he'd always made, artfully woven in with his habitual flattery, stung, like the bites of an invisible insect ("I think it's *interesting* that you pay *so* much more attention to your appearance than you did even just five years ago"). And though I might once have easily brushed them away, suddenly I could not. Nor could I confront him. The conversation moved too quickly.

Q.

When I was nineteen, I had sex with a girl in the public restroom of a club, if you could call that dark, filthy noise pit a club, and we did then. I didn't have to do much to make it happen, so little that I can barely remember. I remember her, though: her small, pretty face too stiff and blank, but her nearly perfect body full of strange, hard will. First I sat and she knelt (shirt pulled up, bra pulled down, amazing breasts popping out, crushed and lopsided), then I stood and she bent, offering herself over a public toilet. We were not alone, the dirty roar of the sound system came in and out with the suctioning door and people spewed into the porcelain pots, crashed around, and laughed in the rattling stalls. She almost ran out when we were done, and, feeling some vague remorse, I asked for her number, because I thought she might want that, though she didn't seem to. I have a photo of a former girlfriend that was taken at the same club; it was taken right as someone pulled up her skirt to show that she wasn't wearing underwear. Her eyes are lowered, her face is turned half defiantly, and her hand is fighting to pull her skirt back down, but she's smiling, and it looks at first glance as if she were the one pulling up her own dress.

I wonder, if those girls were girls now, would they describe themselves as "assaulted" if someone put his hand on their knee? Would they say that they were too "frozen" in dismay to stop him?

What a different story we told about ourselves then. How aware we were that it was a story.

M.

Though they don't often express it freely, some people feel real sympathy for Quin. "It's a travesty," one guy whispered hoarsely over a table during an after-work group drink. "His life is ruined because an *ass* got pinched?" It wasn't just men: a sixty-plus female publicist, who'd been in the business forever, was vocal in her sympathy, calling him "wonderful" and "generous" as her younger colleagues frowned peevishly. "Maybe generous to a fault," she said, "to twits who didn't deserve it, poor man."

The dominant opinion, however, is that he got what he deserved; he'd apparently made more enemies than even I was aware of. Still, most people see my continued friendship with him as loyal, if suspiciously so. My professional reputation, after all, was made when I published a book of charming stories about masochistic women (the now charmless author of which is *still* complaining about the size of her advance), a book that was seen variously as groundbreaking, "empowering," sad, eye-rollingly trite, and, finally, sociologically interesting; although I've shepherded many books into existence since, I have never quite separated myself from that titillating yet tiresome aura. So I took it quite personally when, after a particularly dull conference, gossip turned to all the men who'd recently been exposed and ruined by outraged women, and a colleague said, apropos of what, I don't remember, "Then there's the women trying to defend these creeps. The ones who say, 'That's just what men are like.' Them I feel sorry for. Because I can't imagine what their lives have been like."

She didn't look at me; I didn't look at her. Quin wasn't mentioned by name. Still, I wish I'd said, "Quin isn't 'like' any other man I've met. I don't know any other man as comical and strangely lewd. I don't know any other man who would kneel on the floor of a restaurant and try to kiss your feet just to be whimsical. Or offer to carry your money and lipstick for you, so that you can appear more free. I don't know any other man who would say to a crying woman he barely knew, 'You are a lovely spirit,' and ask her to meet him for tea when her female 'friend' had hung up on her." My very proper colleague would, I'm sure, have hung up too, disgusted by my weakness in that moment. It was Quin who had restored me, and not just on that day. Over days and weeks and months, he helped me feel that I was part of humanity, and not with his kindness alone; it was his silliness, his humor, his *dirtiness* that rekindled my spirit.

I saw him for lunch the other day and he was in exceptionally good form, perfectly dressed, his scarf tasseled rakishly. We talked about books that were coming out, *his* books, one of which had just been very well reviewed in the *Times;* we gossiped about colleagues. We talked about Carolina and about Lucia who, at eight, had suddenly started sucking her thumb, a development that his wife was, he thought, making too much of. He chatted with all the waiters, polling them on everything from their uniforms and how they felt wearing them to their highest hopes and ambitions. The easygoing young men were plainly amused. "Keep asking questions!" one exhorted as we finally made our exit.

"I think things are turning around for me," Quin said. "I can feel it. The city is opening to me again."

Heart pain. Real.

Q.

Stories, it's all stories. Life is too big for anybody, and that's why we invent stories. Women are now very into the victim story; those I've offended are all victims, even as they're feted everywhere. I could make that my story, too, but it's not the best, because it's much too simple. The best story is one that reveals a truth, like something you see and understand in a dream but forget as soon as you wake up. The girl who bent over the toilet for me so long ago—she was acting out a truth that she then ran from, and her running was also true. When I stuck my thumb in that girl's face—the example Margot never ceases to bring up, as if it were the worst outrage of all—I was daring her to show herself, and I was showing myself, too, showing my need to live and feel alive. I was asking, *inviting:* Can you play, do you play? Her answer was no, and that was fine. I bought her book anyway; I even read some of it.

Well, and now the truth is that everyone has said no. Now the truth is that I'm the man in the sexy artist's video, kneeling and barking for a kiss. Really, I've always been him. I would have done anything Sharona wanted—invite her boyfriend to dinner with us, so that I could be in her presence; kneel and bark if it would lead to laughter and a kiss, just a kiss! Well, that all sounds very disingenuous. I can see Margot rolling her eyes. I can see Carolina, her face stunned and desolate, aged by grief—the way she looks when she thinks

I can't see her, the way she looked last night, coming out of Lucia's room, her bright smile collapsing, then hardening as soon as she saw me. I can see my little girl, her lovely cheeks and forehead glowing in the dim light of her laptop behind a half-closed door, carefully not hearing the angry words, the tears. What she might see on that laptop one day: it comes barreling at me with sickening speed, veers malevolently close, then passes like some satanic truck in a horror movie. It's a sad story, all right, but . . . Best to take it one day at a time. And remember . . .

Life is big enough for any story. I walk in the street with tears running down my face; I walk in a world of sales racks and flavored refreshments, marching crowds, broken streets, and steam pouring through the cracks. Jackhammers, roaring buses, women striding into traffic, knifelike in their high, sharp heels, past windows full of faces, products, bright admonishments, light, and dust. Slouching employees smoke in doorways; waiters clear outdoor tables. Eaters lounge before empty plates, legs spread, working their phones. Vividly colored drinks, wine, bread. Flocks of pigeons, a careful rat. At this newsstand, I know the proprietor; he catches my eye and tactfully registers my tears with the slightest change in his expression. Deep in his cave of fevered headlines and gaudy faces, he shivers with cold and fights to breathe; his lungs are failing as he sells magazines and bottled water, mints and little basil plants. We greet each other; I don't say but I think, *Hello, brother.* And life rushes by. On the corner, people play instruments and sing. Sullen men sit with filthy dogs and beg. In the subway, a hawk-nosed boy with dyed, stringy, somehow elegant hair squats and manipulates crude puppets to sexy music amid a weird tableau of old toys. There is something sinister; he looks up with a pale, lewd eye. An older woman laughs too loudly, trying to get his attention. A beggar looks at me and says, "Don't be so sad. It'll get better by and by." And I believe him. There will be something else for me. If not here, then in London, I can feel it. I am on the ground and bleeding, but I will stand up again. I will sing songs of praise.

The beggar laughs behind me, shouts something I can't hear. I turn, a dollar already in my hand.

A Note About the Author

Mary Gaitskill, whose most recent book is *Somebody with a Little Hammer: Essays,* is the author of the story collections *Bad Behavior, Because They Wanted To,* and *Don't Cry,* and of the novels *The Mare, Veronica,* and *Two Girls, Fat and Thin.*

A Note on the Type

This book was set in a version of the well-known Monotype face Bembo. This letter was cut for the celebrated Venetian printer Aldus Manutius by Francesco Griffo, and first used in Pietro Cardinal Bembo's De Aetna of 1495.

Typeset by Scribe,
Philadelphia, Pennsylvania

Printed and bound by LSC Communications,
Harrisonburg, Virginia

Designed by Michael Collica